Experiences from:
The School of Hard Knocks

To Tia & Dan

I wish you all the best that life has to offer.

Love,

Phil Aranuy

Experiences from:
The School of Hard Knocks

By

Gil Francisco

Library of Congress Control Number:	2010910988
ISBN:	Hardcover	978-1-4535-4529-4
	Softcover	978-1-4535-4528-7
	Ebook	978-1-4535-4530-0

This book was printed in the United States of America.

To order additional copies of this book, contact:
Xlibris Corporation
1-888-795-4274
www.Xlibris.com
Orders@Xlibris.com
84417

Introduction

This is a story of an educator. A tough inner-city "kid" who eventually grew to be Principal, a job he never aspired. How life's experiences, the "School of Hard Knocks" and life's peculiar twists of fate somehow predetermined that for short moment in time he would be the head of an urban high school.

This is a story of five encounters on one particular day and how they impacted his life and the lives of teachers, parents and students. Mr. Francisco's flashbacks to his youth on the streets of New York's West Side are amusing and heart piercing. They provide the basis and experience for his problem solving and decision making.

The author questions the over emphasis on acquisition of facts and assessment and the lack of student interaction with ideas and experiences. He questions the lack of development of character in our schools. He advocates student and teacher incentives grounded in effort and productivity.

In the end, we are reminded that life's experiences from the "School of Hard Knocks" often remain with us for a lifetime.

Chapter I

Like Gibran, "I have learned silence from the talkative, toleration from the intolerant and kindness from the unkind"; yet, some may say I was ungrateful to those teachers. But, I never wanted the position. Being the person everyone answered to would remove me from where I felt most productive. I would no longer be able to interact with faculty, staff, parents and students on a level where I felt I could impact the learning process best, unless the role could be redefined. I knew being made principal meant stepping into a world of educational politics. A world where the strings attached to me would be controlled by the politically inclined, the prestige and power driven. Being chief administrator of an urban high school would mean being dictated to by individuals that are often not schooled in education, are often motivated by self-interests and seldom impose decisions that are of any beneficial consequence to the true district and certainly not schooled in the world of "hard knocks". My predecessor was forced to resign. He was knowledgeable and hard working, yet he was rejected because it was someone's pleasure. Knowing my fate would be an "early autumn" as was his, being mid-year I felt compelled to take the job. So began my one-hundred and eighty days.

Walk softly. Carry a big stick and avoid using it. This was the old school philosophy I was groomed in as an educational administrator and it worked well for me. Students and faculty knew I was the man in charge. They didn't need me constantly reminding them of that fact. They knew I was the Principal. "Francisco, how's your wife and my kids?" That was sophomore Billy Duff's way of saying, good morning Mr. Francisco. "My wife is fine and your kids are out to lunch", was my way of saying good morning Mr. Duff. Billy wouldn't have it any other way as he smiled and his friends laughed and slapped five. Every morning Billy greeted me with a "smart" remark and couldn't wait for my retort. I also enjoyed the way classical music greeted me every morning as I walked in the building, it reminded me that I was in a very special place and fortunate to be there.

My daily walk through the building, before teachers and students arrived, would always lead me past memorials, good and bad, of all of the students I loved. Walking past the gym reminded me of all of the championships and hours of commitment students left on the court. However, with all of the glory the gym harnessed, Tyrone's memory was always the first thing I remembered. He was perhaps one of the best all around athletes we had ever seen at Abraham Lincoln High School. Ty had the potential for being an All-State candidate in each one of the four major sports. At five feet eleven inches tall he could dunk a basketball, high jump six feet five inches, throw a football fifty yards and hit a baseball for distance and with consistency. His collapse on our basketball court during an intramural game sent screams throughout the building. Upon my arrival to the gym, I immediately began to assist our athletic trainer and a physical education teacher who had started administering CPR. The EMT's and police arrived within seconds, yet those seconds seemed an eternity. I followed what must have been a twelve car caravan to the emergency unit but Ty was lost in the ambulance.

Moving closer to my office, I walk past the bulletin boards set up to announce student activities. It made me proud to know the students and teachers were getting involved. However, no matter how many successful activities we executed every year, the one that ended in tragedy always comes into my mind. Would Ronda's brilliance have led her to the worlds of medicine, law or education? Would her beauty and talent have led her to the world of fine arts? The struggle to release her from the invisible force that had suctioned her to the bottom of the "hot tub" was relentless. Students frantically began to bail water as another administrator, a policeman and I attempted to bring her to the surface but to no avail. Her hand, her left hand, that I saw for months in my dreams was the only part of her body that we could bring to the surface. Ironically, we had scheduled the after-prom to keep the students safe and off the roads. We had taken all precautions to assure everyone's safety but a crack in the grill at the bottom of the "hot-tub" had gone undetected by inspectors at a local health club. Months later after investigations were complete, it was determined that the force of several elephants had Ronda pinned to the bottom of the tub.

I often think of what would have become of Ronda and Tyrone. They were two wonderful students whose lives were accidently ended. They demonstrated so much potential and promise but their brilliant flames flickered and expired much too early. No graduate school course can ever prepare you for the loss of a child left in your care. Yet, each day brought new promise, new expectations along with problems and decision making.

Danny Villanueva and his mother rushed into the main office that morning and sat anxiously awaiting my arrival. Seldom does a student drag a parent to the principal's office. It is usually the other way around. Danny was convinced, by some students he had recently met, that if there was someone who could get him off a hit list it was the Principal.

My quarter century of living and working in the community and being involved with parents and older brothers and sisters had earned the student's trust and respect. I was so very proud of that.

The Villanueva family had moved down from the City to get Danny away from the gangs, drugs and overall violence that had taken over many of the inner city neighborhoods. The problem in jumping from one town to the next is; you can't run away from yourself. Moving into what he thought was the "sticks", Danny Villanueva arrived in his new neighborhood and high school with a chip on his shoulder. Very quickly, Danny found out he could get shot-up in "Anytown USA" as easily as he could in "Anyhood USA" across the country. Danny's parents didn't realize their cherished son was very much a part of the problems they were trying to protect him from. The Villanuevas, like many parents, just didn't know the signs of gang involvement. The parents thought Danny's tattoos and style of dress were simply a fad he was going through. Mrs. Villanueva was very much aware of the threat against her son's life and was wondering why she was sitting distraught outside the principal's office and not at police headquarters filing a report. Danny Villanueva, "Hard Hands" in Brooklyn, feared "snitches get stitches" or worse, so he begged his mom to try this option first. Villanueva understood his world very well. He had made a comment about a local gang being a bunch of punks and the comment was caught on cell phone. Not knowing who these guys were, how they were connected or what they were capable of, Danny shot his mouth off and was going to pay the price, it was a matter of respect. As I walked in, I glanced at Danny. A look of desperation was written on his face. Before I could get a word out, Mrs. Villanueva angrily yelled; "a bunch of punks in this poor excuse of a high school are threatening my son". "Mrs. Villanueva, please come in my office. I will do everything I possibly can to make sure your son is not harmed by anyone". I knew it wasn't only anger but frustration and fear spouting from Mrs. Villanueva, the ultimate fear for any parent, the thought of burying a child. In recent years, I had become far too familiar with the anguished looks and primal screams of parents losing a child to gang violence. I was, as I have been on many occasions, the sounding board for a desperate parent. So her words did not anger or offend me but brought out a sense of compassion. I asked Danny for a copy of the recording and to my surprise he had it in his pocket. After playing the cell phone recording, I realized his words had not only offended suspected students at the high school but an older group they were being controlled by, it was the older crew he really had to fear. I assured both Danny and Mrs. Villanueva of the seriousness of this situation. I asked Danny what made him come to me first; he responded, "you know them, they went to school here, everyone says you're the only one they might listen to, or so my friends tell me".

The members of the Jazz Band were also sitting in the outer office that particular morning. Their world was completely different from Danny Villanueva's world but their need appeared as urgent. The musical piece they were assigned for the spring concert was Afro-Blue, the Mongo Santamaria composition. The spring concert was the culminating activity that would highlight a year's hard work, sacrifice and musical development. With a good horn section and a talented young lady named Giovanna on the vibes, the Cal Tjader arrangement was the logical choice. However, there was a minor problem which was a major problem. The rhythm section had no one who could play the conga drums. A Mongo Santamaria piece without a conga was like showing up at a dance and no girls, what's the point. I was in the habit of occasionally calling members of the group out of class whenever I remembered a piece that featured an instrument they played. Vinnie Tavares played the flute and alto sax. Introducing Vinnie to Dave Valentine, Paquito D'Rivera and some of the old Cuban Masters, while at the same time watching his progress, brought great satisfaction to my otherwise hectic daily routine. One afternoon I played Tito Puente's version of the Miles Davis classic, Milestones. Danny sat mesmerized. All he could say was, "that shit was hot!" He quickly apologized for the slip of the tongue. I said, "no, no don't apologize. Tito Puente, Dave Valentine, Paquito D'Rivera, Mario Rivera, Mongo Santamaria together at the Village Gate, that shit was real hot!" I remember Vinnie's mother cornering me at the local pizza shop and telling me the Afro-Cuban Jazz I was introducing her son to was driving her crazy, "he plays it night and day". My response was; "did you know Cole Porter wrote, Night and Day?" She looked at me as though I was crazy. Ian Cummings was simply musically gifted. Piano, sax and percussion were all part of his arsenal. Yet, it was playing the bass that really touched his soul. Ian's visits to my office consisted of mini sessions listening to the likes of Ray Brown, Charlie Mingus and Israel Lopez "Cachao". During these impromptu visits to the principal's office the members of the Jazz Band could not help but notice the conga drum standing in the corner. Teachers who had stopped by my home during the holidays for a small faculty get-together had leaked information to the band members that I could play.

Those two conferences that morning resulted in me re-entering two worlds that were completely different from each other but very familiar, I had been there. I couldn't help reflecting back to my own youth and how similar situations were now playing out for me as principal of Abraham Lincoln High School.

Mine was the best of worlds, it was the worst, and it's still mine. That is, my heart has never left it. Central Park, The

Museum of Natural History, Columbia University, The Cathedral of Saint John the Divine were all right there, "a one handed catch". Stickball, home-made scooters, doo wops lit up every block, but, so did gangs, guns, heroine and hookers offering "half and halves", they too were a one-handed catch. It was the best of times and the most horrible of times. The golden ages of Television, Baseball and Broadway were at their peaks and it seems that it was not so long ago or so far away. Little did we know that a play written about our neighborhood, at the time we were growing up, would become immortal. The rumble scene seemed corny. Hey, at least they hired some of the older guys from the neighborhood for crowd control was our attitude. It wasn't until later that we realized Laurents, Bernstein, Sondheim, Wise and Robbins had put together a masterpiece, a tale of love, conflicts and survival. The creators of West Side Story were aiming at a modern day Romeo and Juliet, but they told it like it was in our place and time. They got it right. Yet, among all the culture, Father Knows Best and the World Series, which seemed to play out every year in New York, drugs and gang violence were killing us. Nobody Cared. Pimps and pushers carried out their trade and it was "ok", as long as it was kept in certain areas. Manhattan Valley, the area from 96st to 110st east of Broadway to Central Park West, was one of those areas. Through it all, and most important, it was my time and place.

That time and place was The West Side, abundant with landmarks and still is. The "real" land marks are gone. Commerce High School where Lou Gehrig, George Gershwin, Cal Ramsey, Louis Lefkowitz and so many prominent others attended no longer stands. Power Memorial High School, the home of Kareem Abdul Jabbar a.k.a. Lew Alcindor, has also given way to a high-rise. The original Victor's Café is no longer on 71st, it has moved to the theatre district. What a great hang-out it was for my god-father and his friends. I am sure

106st (Duke Ellington Blvd) will endure. The Ansonia Hotel where the likes of Caruso and Toscanini resided, as well as the place where the 1919 Black Sox Scandal was conceived, will also endure.

There are the personal spots that will endure because they will forever be etched in my mind. 86th and Broadway where Bobby was killed by a cab was one of those spots. Bobby was on his way to pick up our baseball uniforms when his uncle's car was rear ended and completely demolished. I was supposed to be in that car. An errand I had to run for my grandmother probably saved my life. I have often thought about how a slight delay, such as taking time allowing me to run an errand may have altered that incident. Riverside Drive, by the tracks, where Neno over-dosed (his body found a week later eaten by rats) is another spot. Neno was gifted in science and math. He got himself mixed up with a crew from the east side. He finally couldn't keep up with his habit. The money he owed was impossible to make good on. They finally gave him a hot dose to make it look like an over dose and at the same time send a message. Cathedral Parkway where I got my ass kicked by Billy Betancourt and the Tunney Twins is also indelible. Those guys hated my ass and I hated them right back. A week later my friends and I caught Phil Tunney coming out of the 96st subway station and he got his. Then there was 108st between Manhattan Avenue and Central Park West, where the egg creams in Moe's Candy Store, the smell of hot starch from the Chinese Laundry and the Opera music from the cobbler's shop gave 108st a special charm. Manhattan Avenue and Central Park West were two completely different worlds, although only two hundred yards apart. Poor Whites, Blacks and Hispanics who had to struggle to make ends meet lived on Manhattan Avenue and on 108st. But, once you turned the corner on to Central Park West you stepped into a world of affluence, comfort and privilege. Drugs, guns, prostitution and the "numbers" were forbidden. As strange as it may sound, the charm of 108st is something I would not have traded for back then or even now.

Those "balmy breezes" Lorentz Hart wrote about charmed me one afternoon as I stepped out of the subway on to Cathedral Parkway. The trees in the park knew it was their time of year to show off, turning crimson, canary and gold. It was like nature holding its' own Mardi Gras. Nature was anxious that year, it was an "early autumn". I turned down 108st, between Manhattan and Central Park West. Although these two avenues were worlds apart, the "have nots" and the "haves", no other street compared to 108st, no, not even Mott street.

It was late afternoon and the push-carts, ice cream wagons and horse-drawn veggie stands had started their daily parade down the block. And there they were, my boys, in their usual poses sitting on the stoop, leaning on parked cars and smoking by the lamp post. But, something was wrong. I could feel it. You could cut the tension with a switch-blade. Just then Billy "Cow Ass" spotted me and yelled, "Hey Frankie, the shit is on!" That meant only one thing, a fight. We called him Cow Ass because he had the biggest and highest ass we had ever seen on a human being. Billy Cow Ass and his older sister Maxine were very angry and had plenty to be angry about. Billy and Maxine lost their Dad in the Korean Conflict and their mom shacked up with a local pimp named Jimmy. Jimmy the Pimp would beat on Billy just for practice. Maxine, whom as a child was your classic tom-boy, had now blossomed into a gorgeous woman. Jimmy the Pimp had her turning "tricks" behind the Four Seasons Barbershop. Billy's mom along with the Pimp, decided to get drunk one night and take a drive through Central Park. The car was found in flames with both bodies burned beyond recognition. Maxine took over the Pimp's business and Cow Ass lived on the streets. Sitting next to him was "Uncle Baggy". In an era when teenagers wore tight dungarees with thick garrison belts, this guy wore pants that looked like trash bags. Leaning on a Chevy were Todd and Ditzie, these two were inseparable. All they did was goof on each other's mother. No matter where or when, they goofed on each other's mom. The looks on all their faces that day, was serious. Some guys from 100st had "cocktailed" Moe's Candy Store, our hang-out. Ditzie said Todd's mother was selling pussy on 100st and that's why they came around. We cracked-up laughing, but soon the mood, again, grew tense.

We didn't consider ourselves a gang but the reality was, we were. We were organized, we had a hierarchy and we were loyal to each other, just like gangs today. It amazes me when people ask; why do kids join gangs? The answer has been the same since the first teenage gangs appeared in Five Points 100 years ago. Poverty! Poverty breeds despair, broken homes, single families and homelessness. Poverty breeds a desire to belong, boredom and want. Poverty breeds an anger that makes a youth not care. Always be careful of the one who doesn't care, he seeks nothing and will do anything for the sake of doing it. If you want to reduce gangs, give these kids a reason not to join one.

The tense moment grew into a want for revenge, the most senseless of causes. The decision was made without discussion, we would call them out. It didn't matter where, Central Park, Riverside Drive, under the Highway or the playground. They had to be taught a lesson.

The cops in those days walked the beat, took no shit and taught lessons of their own. Officer John Doherty walked the beat between 106st and 110st on Manhattan Avenue. We nicknamed him "Little John", because he was the biggest son-of-bitch you'd ever want to meet and one swing from his night stick was lethal. One day he kicked the crap out of three dealers who had come up from Hell's Kitchen to sell heroine. We never knew how tough Little John really was. After the ambulance carted the "pushers" away we knew. We knew we could never fuck with Little John. Besides working for the City of New York, Little John worked for Anthony "Fat Tony" Nitali. You see, Tony ran the neighborhood and it was John Doherty's job to keep it clean of outsiders; no drugs! Gambling, women, numbers only with Tony's say so, were allowed. It wasn't like Little John was on the take in the true sense of the phrase. John Doherty and Tony Nitali grew up together and were the best of friends. They went to Dewitt Clinton High School back when Clinton was still on the West Side. Story says Tony once took a bullet for John. Life dealt each of them a different hand, Tony became connected to one of the five families which ran New York and John became a cop. However, their loyalty to each other was never questioned. They were like Cagney and O'Brien in "Angels with Dirty Faces". In their own ways these guys knew people, especially kids. They knew how to get to your mind. They knew how to get to your heart. Tony always said, "it's not the song, it's how you feel about it". What great educators Doherty and Nitali would have made. They knew the secret; understand what a kid feels, how he thinks and you can teach him anything.

Little John's world was different from mine but we had one thing in common, Baseball. We loved Baseball. Like me, he ate, slept and shit Yankee Pinstripes. Mantle, Maris, Berra and Ford were our connection into that world most appreciated but few lived for. Baseball is short lived. Yet, nothing teaches the game of life, mirroring the ups and downs, like a ball, a bat and a glove. John Doherty signed a pro contract right out of high school but soon after blew his arm out. Officer John twirled his night stick like no other; he had hands like Clete

Boyer. He walked towards us, stopped and looked me dead in the eye. I knew my response had to be as fast as he posed the questions.

Little John—What is Yogi's real name?
Frankie—Lawrence
Little John—Where was the Mick Born?
Frankie—Commerce, Oklahoma
Little John—Who holds the Yankee record for stolen bases?

Todd said, "Ditzie's mother". His timing was perfect. We busted out laughing. Like natural comedians, Todd and Ditzie's one liners were always on cue. It got me off the hook. I didn't know the answer. The big cop took a few steps down the block, stopped, turned and said, "the guys from 100st are pretty good stick-ball players", then walked away. We froze. Time froze. Then with the acapela harmony of Dion and the Belmonts we said, "Oh shit, he knows". He saw vengeance written on our faces and as he always did Officer John Doherty was sending us a message. The message was clear. He didn't want anything coming down on his beat. John also knew that for us, it was a matter of respect. Somehow we had to face off with the boys of 100st.

But, a stick-ball game, we'll be laughed right out of the West Side. Was he really suggesting a stick-ball game? These guys cocktailed Moe's Candy Store! These were the thoughts running through our minds. Most importantly, if Little John Doherty knew, Anthony Fat Tony Nitali knew.

Tony's first love was not baseball, women or even money, his world was Jazz. He loved how jazz artist would interpret what we call today American Songbook. As for the writers he loved Gershwin, Ellington and Porter. Coltrane, Parker, Sinatra and Ella were his top performers. He constantly reminded us, how the groups of the fifties and early sixties couldn't come close to Sinatra. Yet, he would love to hear us sing. It didn't matter where we sang. Hallways, tunnels, rooftops; Nitali would always come hear us sing. Tony didn't want a rumble, it was bad for business. His message was also clear, find another way to settle it. But, who would offer the challenge. Todd and Ditzie would offer each others' mother. Cow Ass had a bad temper and a fight would break out right then and there. Uncle Baggy, would forget what the deal was by the time he reached 100st. War councils were dangerous. The challenge had to be made on the other gangs turf. Yet, this challenge was different. It was a stickball game in place of a rumble and no one wanted to make the challenge. Butchy and Melvin, Jug Head, Peg Leg all said they would play the game but not offer the challenge. We needed someone who was feared and commanded respect, someone who could guarantee the agreement on both sides. The more I thought about it, the answer became clear as a bell. Little John, yeah, Officer John Doherty, he wanted a stickball game he should set it up. It made sense to all of us but how would we get him to do it?

Joe Nitali was Tony's son, my next door neighbor and best friend. I whistled for him and he came to the window. I said, "meet me on the roof". Joe flew pigeons and he was always up on the roof. The Drifters knew what they were singing about. Plans were made, crap games played and virginity was lost, "Up on the Roof". Before I could utter a word, Joe said, "Doherty has to make the deal". Joe said, "Think about it, Little John knows, that means all the cops know. My old man knows, that means the Bosses know. Most of all, the guys from 100st can't back down. For them it means play or get pinched for what they did to Moe's Candy Store". The challenge now became getting a decorated veteran who had turned down promotions within the NYPD to arrange a stickball game. Joe said, "pop him a baseball question he can't answer. Now he owes you". We grew up in a world of deals and bets but not favors. No one did something for nothing. Then it hit me, who the hell knows who holds the record for the most stolen bases as a Yankee. I waited for him to step out of Lou's Deli where he was polishing off a corned-beef sandwich. "Officer Doherty", I yelled. No one called him Little John to his face, (You Kiddin). "I got one for you. But, if you miss, you've got to do something for me and the boys". He said, "that depends, give it to me anyway". "Who holds the record for most stolen bases as a Yankee?" All he could do was smile. I knew he was thinking of Todd's answer the day he threw that same question at me. I stumped him! He said, "you and the boys meet me at Moe's at closing". Suddenly his facial expression changed. He gave me the "Look". If you did something wrong in my neighborhood the adults would give you, The Look. The Look could make you un-ball your fist. The Look could make you stain your Fruit of the Looms right on the spot. My mother knew how to give, The Look. Whenever I stepped out of line I got that cold chilling stare. She's in heaven now and how I miss, her Look. In this case, The Look meant we better be there.

Autumn afternoons were warm as toast but once the sun went down we wore our black satin jackets with red trim. Moe started pulling down the gates when Doherty pulled up in an unmarked car. Unmarked cars were always these beat-up Fords. Anyone who owned a car in our neighborhood kept it nice. I never understood why the cops even bothered. Anyway, the line, "make them an offer they can't refuse" hadn't been coined yet but that was basically what Little John gave the boys from 100st. The shit was really on. Doherty said, "sit down and don't say a word". No one spoke, not even Todd and Ditzie. We got The Look, then Little John said, "BASIC RULES"

- On a roof is automatically out.
- Everything else is playable.
- Down a cellar is a ground-rule double.
- Three sewers is a homerun.
- Five innings.
- No ringers from another block.
- Winners extend their turf.
- Losers stay on their turf.
- Oh, I'm the ump!

The game was set for Saturday afternoon at 2 o'clock on 106st between Manhattan Avenue and Central Park West. Today that spot is called Duke Ellington Boulevard, after the great band leader, musician and composer. Stories about the West Side and the famous people that lived there in the twenties, thirties and forties abound. George Gershwin wrote his famous Rhapsody in Blue in his 110st apartment. Lou Gehrig lived on 112st between Amsterdam and Broadway while he attended Columbia. The "Babe", George Herman Ruth lived in the Ansonia Hotel before he moved to Riverside Drive. And of course, Edwin "Duke" Ellington was inspired and wrote many of his songs while living on 106st near Riverside Drive.

106st between Manhattan and Central Park West was not only a neutral block but a two-way street. This gave us more space for the game and plenty of room for spectators. This was the first of its kind, a stickball game instead of bustin' heads. Officer Doherty even had the street closed to traffic. This idea that seemed as corny as Russ Tamblyn and George Chikaris dancing through the rumble scene a few months earlier, during the taping of West Side Story, suddenly took on a life of its own. Parents were talking about it. Store owners were talking about it. Even the girls were talking about it. That night Joe and I went up on the roof, to choose the players and set our line-up. Ditzie would pitch and Todd would catch. They were the perfect battery. We knew their constant bullshit would either make the other team laugh or piss them off. Regardless, their focus and concentration would be gone. Plus, Ditzie could put a spin on a "Spaldeen" that broke sharper than Whitey Ford's curve ball. Cow Ass would play first base. Uncle Baggy would play third base, right next to the "Johnny Pump" and in front of the nursing home. Joe, Billy Boy, and I would play the outfield spots. We were the best at playing balls off the fire escapes and parked cars. The stage was set.

It was a clear, brisk day. We waited in Central Park until we got word the boys from 100st had arrived. The word came. We jumped over Central Park Wall wearing our jackets. We strutted down the center of 106st tapping our stickball bats in unison. Word about the game had spread and people came from all over. All the cops assigned to juvenile were there; "Bat Man and Robin", "Jimmy Cagney" and "Friday" were there. Fat Tony, Father Bagley and Moe showed up. People were yelling from the windows and the fire escapes. Over 100 people had lined the sidewalks to watch. The Yanks had just beaten the Giants in the World Series and this was like our own game seven, winners take all. Doherty flipped a coin. Joe called heads. It was heads and we took the field. Their first batter was a guy called "Lippo". Todd yelled to Ditzie, "look at the lips on this mother fucker!" He must have sucked the shit out of your mother's tit last night". The crowd busted out laughing. Lippo went after Todd but Doherty stepped in and broke it up. "Knock it off, let's play ball". That kid should have sat down and watched. He was so pissed he couldn't hit a beach ball. Carmine, their leader, yelled out to Ditzie, "hey Ditz, I was with your moms last night". Ditzie yelled back, "I know, she said forty seconds and you were done!" The game hadn't started and Todd and Ditzie had the crowd in "stitches". By the third inning we had a four nothin' lead and the guys from 100st. had enough of Todd and Ditzie. Carmine screamed out; "why don't you guys shut the fuck up?" Our strategy had worked. The last thing on their minds was the game. They just wanted to kick the shit out of Todd and Ditzie. A classic game was played and it was now the last inning and the score was tied. Fortunately, Joe won the coin toss at the beginning of the game and he chose to take the field giving us "last licks". We second guessed Joe when he wrote down the batting order, batting me lead off instead of fourth. He looked at us and said; "This is neighborhood stickball, not baseball". His reasoning was that the best hitter should have the most at bats. Joe was right. I led off the bottom of the fifth instead of being scheduled to hit fourth that inning. Carmine was their pitcher and a lefty at that. Carmine's spinner was jamming me all game. As I stepped up to the manhole cover (sewer) Little John casually whispered, "Step back off the plate". I smoked the first pitch out on to the avenue. The ball hit the number 10 bus which runs along Central Park West. The place went wild! We had just won our own version of the "Fall Classic" and we felt like Kings. The boys from 100st started walking home but they had nothing to be ashamed of. The crowd gave them an ovation, it was a great game and most importantly the rumble problem was solved. In fact, we got along with the boys from 100st after that Saturday afternoon. There were many heroes that day in 1962, but as the years passed I realized the true hero was Officer Little John Doherty.

Like Doherty had done forty-five years earlier, I found myself going into the "belly of the beast", but this time searching out two guys in their early twenties that I had known since they were ten years old. Both were born and raised in town. They had played Little League and Bitty Basketball for me and for a while were friends with my son.

Family trips to nearby amusement parks and family outings often included Teddy and Lamar. I couldn't help but think of the horrible twists of fate they had each gone through. Parents lost to violence, drug addiction, child abuse and multiple arrests highlighted their resumes. My presence on Malcolm X Blvd was not uncommon. Between home visits and placing students on home intervention, my figure was a common sight. Those that needed to know who was on the block at all times, knew that I was present and in a short while both young men I was hoping to run into, found me. Teddy and Lamar's smiles were genuine as were the hugs we exchanged. I hadn't seen them in several years and the hardness they had to bear in those years had now become part of their persona. The innocence, joy and promise I had often seen on their faces as little boys had been replaced by an angry, callous demeanor. "Please give Danny Villanueva a pass". They gave me The Look, a cold stare, a stare that pierced through me, a stare that let me know that I may have crossed their line. "Remember the Roberto Clemente Summer League you started for us"? I replied, "How can I forget"? I followed their flow with the rapid change in subject and continued to reminisce. We talked about their days at the high school and went as far back as their skinny dipping escapade at an Atlanta hotel during a national tournament when they were kids. I left the two young men not knowing whether my mission to help Danny Villanueva was successful or an exercise in futility. The following morning I found a note in my mailbox which simply said, "It's all good". For safe measure, I informed our Resource Officer about what had transpired and we placed a "tag" on Danny Villanueva. A plain clothed security guard had Danny in sight for a week. Two weeks later Danny Villanueva transferred out of Abraham Lincoln High School. I don't know whether the threat against Danny "Hard Hands" Villanueva would have been executed or whether I had touched a chord with two former ball players who had been dealt an unfortunate hand so early in life. All I know is that I had drawn my strength from a New York City Police Officer who served as a role model forty-five years earlier and never asked for anything in return. A year later both young men were charged with a shooting, unconnected with Danny Villanueva.

As a result of that game, stickball teams sprung up all over the West Side. The 24th precinct started a summer stickball league which ran for several years.

Years later, Carmine and I found ourselves playing on the same high school and college teams. As all the guys from the neighborhood went their separate ways, we were given a financial incentive and took advantage of it. We left the City to play college ball in Kansas.

Todd and Ditzie attended City College where they majored in English. I later found out they had moved to the west coast and became comedy writers.

Uncle Baggy got his degree in education at St. John's University. Today he teaches Physical Education.

Cow Ass joined the Marines and in a fate similar to his father's was killed in action in Viet Nam.

Fat Tony Nitali was shot and killed during a crap game. They said it was an argument over money, it was really a hit. The Bosses wanted to open up the neighborhood to drugs and Tony was in the way. The Nitali's moved and I never saw or heard from them again.

Officer "Little John" Doherty retired from the NYPD and moved to Ireland where he opened up his own Pub. One day I received a package in the mail, it was his Night Stick.

Oh yeah, in 1962 the record for the most stolen bases by a New York Yankee was held by Hal Chase.

Forty-five years later I tried to introduce Program Night Stick, an initiative to help bring gang awareness to the community and several youth agencies were ready to come on board. Evening tutoring, family services, fine arts programs, technology programs and recreational programs were designed to keep teens off the streets. The initiative was shot down by the power elite, as gangs were not a problem that directly affected their community and thus not a funding priority.

Chapter II

I knew how the High School Jazz Band felt about Afro-Blue, we shared the same love. The composition had grown on each and every one of us. We could feel the energy on stage whenever we practiced the piece. I say we because the Jazz Band had honored me by requesting that I sit in as their guest artist for the performance. I had taken batting practice with the baseball team, filled in as goalie for the girls soccer team during one of their practice sessions, hit with the tennis team, but this was the real deal. I was asked to be a part of their spring concert.

Ad Deum qui lae ti fi cat juven tu tem me am (I go to the altar of God, the God who gives joy to my youth). This was the opening to the prayers at the foot of the altar. These words we recited hundreds of times. Believe it or not, we were altar boys. It was the price we paid in order to learn how to sing. We knew sports and entertainment were our tickets out of what was a violence infested ghetto but what today I cherish most, memories of the West Side. So we decided to start a singing group. Acapella was the sound of the fifties and early sixties; much like hip-hop is today. Some of the older guys from the West Side and Harlem had made it, so we decided to give it a shot. There was one problem; we didn't know how to sing. Back then the mass was recited in Latin and the High Mass was sung in Latin. Altar boys were not only taught Latin but they spent hours learning how to sing. So Joe and I decided to sign up. Father Bagley taught us Latin and Professor McNulty taught us how to sing. Bagley was your classic, tough parish priest. He could and did "mix it up" with anybody. He did however, have this knack for tripping on the steps of the altar. We nicknamed him "Father Oops". Guys that we thought were "soft" and often picked on, suddenly became our friends and we didn't let anyone mess with them. In fact, we made Butchy and Melvin join after we caught them trying to shake down some of the other altar boys. Suddenly the altar boys had respect and everyone wanted to join. Johnny T. had a voice like an angel, high and with perfect pitch. Carlton had the voice of man and sang with the baritones. After finally learning how to hold a note, McNulty made Joe and me tenors. Johnny, Carlton Joe and I became the High Notes mainly because of the high falsetto notes Johnny could hit. We had lessons with McNulty twice a week and we sang on our own every other day. We sang anywhere we could get an echo; hallways, subway stations along Central Park West and the tunnels along Riverside Drive. The tunnels along Riverside Drive were our favorite spots, they were the only places we wouldn't get kicked out of. After several months we noticed people would stop and listen. Stormy Weather, That's My Desire, Zoom Zoom Zoom and "My Girl Friend" became our early repertoire. There was an older guy named Tom who would come around whenever we sang in the late afternoon near 110th street and Riverside Drive. Tom was a great source of encouragement. We didn't know who he was or what he did for a living but we knew it had something to do with music. The pointers Tom gave us on staying on key and where to go up half a step gave us a sound that finally introduced us to CYO dances, parties and girls, girls who brought "joy to my youth". These girls were all over us, even at Sunday Mass they would smile or give us a wink. It was right after an 11 o'clock Mass, in the basement of the CYO center, that Pookie Martinez introduced me to "Suckin' Face" (Making Out). It was heaven! I swore right then and there, I would throw away the Playboy Magazines I had hidden in the bathroom wall.

Singing gave us our first real introduction to racism and it was right across the George Washington Bridge. We started getting gigs on a regular basis and we changed our name to "Joe Vitali and The High Notes". We didn't have a problem with Joe being the headliner. After all, his father Tony backed us whenever we needed money for jackets, ties or car fare. No one in Manhattan cared about us being a racially mixed group. Joe was Italian, Carlton was Black, Johnny and I were Latino. Without giving it a thought when we put the group together, we were a true representation of what the West Side had become by the early 1960's. In Fort Lee we were booked sight unseen, just on our reputation. With Joe Nitali being the headliner they assumed they were getting an all Italian singing group. We arrived and the "shit hit the fan". "Who the fuck booked niggers and spics"? These cocksuckers aren't singing to our kids". Growing up on the West Side we had heard it all but that really came from the heart. I'll never forget those words or the hatred in the eyes of the man who said them. This guy, who was in his thirties, would have shot us on the spot if he thought he could get away with it. Suddenly, everyone in the dance hall rushed to the entrance where we were and had all but shit our pants. The girls wanted to hear us and were yelling, "let 'em sing". The guys wanted to kick the crap out of us. Joe caught the brunt of their wrath. They started calling him, "nigger lover". Joe had balls. He was the only one that spoke up. Joe just kept saying, "that's right, that's right". Suddenly, a priest showed up and everyone quieted down. The priest asked us if we were Father Bagley's boys. We must have said yes. Who knows? We were too scared to remember who the hell we were. The priest turned to the mob of teenagers and said, "I booked them". No one said shit, not even the fat guy with the cold eyes who greeted us at the door. This priest had their hearts and our asses in the palm of his hand.

Adults back in the fifties and sixties must have all practiced The Look, because this priest gave us The Look and said; "do you guys want to sing?" Of course we said "yes" not because we wanted to but because his Look came with a "Step". The priest's "Look and Step" scared us into doing the right thing, sing like we were hired to do. So he led us to the stage.

The building was your typical "Cafegymitorium", that all purpose building found in parishes in the northeast but the stage was different. The stage was a high, circular, mobile platform the perfect venue today but very uncommon back then; that meant we were completely surrounded by the audience as we performed. What is typically a performers dream was a nightmare for us. Anyone could sneak up behind us while we were singing and we wouldn't see a smack, a punch or even a chair coming. They gave us wired microphones which meant we could move. Joe said, "keep moving while you sing, don't turn your backs on anybody". That's exactly what we did. We had never harmonized on the move before. We always had stand-up microphones and we were stationary. We performed all up tempo songs which added to the precautionary moving about the stage. We were a hit! Fear and creativity on the spot made these kids, who had been taught to hate, judge us for those forty-five minutes for how we sounded, not for how we looked or who we were. Once the set was done we got the hell out of there. The priest gave Joe an envelope, we jumped on a bus and it was back to the sweet sounds of fire engines, sirens and subways on the West Side. The next morning Joe and I reported to serve the nine o'clock mass. Father Bagley asked us how it went. We gave it to him straight. A priest with a Look and Step saved our lives. Bagley simply said; "you didn't feel so tough did you? That priest was my brother". Both priests knew what would happen and they planned it that way. We needed a lesson from the Streets of Hard Knocks and so did those kids from Fort Lee. From that experience we toned down how we walked around and treated people.

Singing acapella was now in our blood. We continued singing whenever and wherever we could. However, we had not built up the courage to go downtown and sing in front of the Brill Building. The Brill was where groups, accidently but on purpose, auditioned. Groups were discovered singing outside the Brill Building. Song writers, agents and other artists were constantly walking in and out. We thought that maybe, just maybe we would catch someone's ear. The Brill Building is one of the most unsung historical sites in New York City. Intended to be a financial building, the Depression forced the owners to explore other means of income so they rented space to members of the music industry. During the big band era Benny Goodman, Glenn Miller and the Dorsey's had their songs "plugged" at the Brill Building. Writers such as Burt Bacharach, Neil Diamond and Carol King worked out of the Brill in the 50's and 60's. In the words of Carol King, "the pressure of the Brill was really terrific".

Pressure brings the best out of people. Pressure to succeed brought out the courage in us to sing in front of this building. We hopped on the number 1 train and headed downtown. We started warming up on the subway platform but the conductor told us to "shut the hell up". We told him to "fuck off" and ran up the stairs and on to the street. We finally got to the Brill Building and just as we were about to do our thing we spotted Tom. Tom, who had been giving us pointers all along, gave us news that broke our hearts. Tom looked at us and in an almost apologetic way said, "Doo Wops are done". We couldn't believe what he said. "What do you mean, how do you know "? Tom just shook his head, said there is a new sound coming in and walked in to the Brill Building. We didn't know what to believe. We sang one song and a cop chased us away. Two weeks later we found out what Tom was talking about. The British Invasion had hit and that's all you heard on radio. The Beatles, The Stones and The Animals were now the sound. Over night The Teenagers, The Cadillacs and The Dubs were a thing of the past. As for us, we were done. Sure, everyone said change your style, but like Tony said, "It's not the song; it's how you feel about it".

It was amazing how music could change a neighborhood, or so it seemed. Long hair and Afros were everywhere. Girls traded in their Poodle Skirts and Saddle Shoes for Mini Skirts and Boots. Drugs were as easy to find as a bottle of Pepsi, especially after Fat Tony was killed. Tony wanted no drugs in his neighborhood and because of that he paid the price. There is a line from "The Godfather" that really hits home, "keep it among the blacks, let them lose their souls". I really feel some neighborhoods were targeted for drugs and ours was one. Once you hit the corner of Central Park West or the corner of West End Avenue things were as clean as a whistle.

Music remained a major interest but my friends and I gravitated towards Latin and Jazz, unusual for kids in their early teens. Latin and jazz grew on us as quickly as the doo wops did, mainly through a DJ named Symphony Sid. Sid's show featured all the Jazz greats Bird, Dizzy, Duke, Count, Ella, Miles, Louie for one hour and the great Latin artists the next hour, Machito and Graciela, Tito Puente, Tito Rodriguez, Celia Cruz, the fabulous list goes on. "Symphony Sid" Torin's show received much criticism for mixing Jazz and Latin. In fact, he was dubbed the "jazz traitor". History now remembers his concept as very important in the evolution of Jazz and Afro-Cuban rhythms in America. Many of these greats not only lived in Manhattan, but on the West Side. Seeing Tito Puente leave his Park West Village apartment or Graciela leave her 106st and Columbus Avenue apartment was as common as seeing an ice cream vendor on Broadway. So our escapades now shifted. We sneaked in and got kicked out of every Jazz and Latin spot in Manhattan; the bouncers at The Village Gate, The Vanguard, Riverside Plaza, The Corso, all left their shoe imprints right between our back pockets. The Metropole's stage in those days was not far from the entrance and we would spend time walking back and forth just to get a glimpse of Gene Krupa who was often featured. We became more sophisticated in our approach and we would get to these clubs early and help the musicians carry their instruments. The Joe Cuba Sextet, I remember as being the coolest group of all, they even showed us where to "lay low" at the Riverside Plaza, right on the fire-escape behind the back stage curtain. Our most memorable day was at the Copa. While sneaking down the back stairs that led to the kitchen, there were the Temptations practicing harmony right in the stairwell. No recording, no wires, no microphones, just their pure voices. For weeks my mind would go back to hearing, "Hello young lovers wherever you are, hello, hello". Of course we were discovered and kicked out; but those three minutes seemed like an eternity. If there is a heaven, the Original Temptations must be there. Music was and still is a major part of my life, all music. It's not the genre, it's the song and how you feel about it.

The Abraham Lincoln High School Band and I practiced every Tuesday and Thursday night leading up to the week before the concert and every night the week before. The thrill of feeling the number come together was exciting. It was as exciting as hearing an acapella harmony come together when I was a kid singing with the High Notes. The word got out about the piece we were playing and members of the concert band decided that playing jazz was not such a bad thing and joined. The jazz band had now grown to a full orchestra. Mrs. Neri, the music director and I scheduled a trip to Lincoln Center. Seeing Arturo O'Farrill and The Lincoln Center Afro Latin Jazz Orchestra gave everyone a feel for what we needed to accomplish and an experience we would never forget.

Ian on bass was the driving force, so the piece opened with his pulsating rhythm. I followed with your standard Afro Cuban beat on the conga. When Giovanna came in on the vibes, the auditorium crowd was brought to their feet. Solos on the flute and sax by Vinnie and Peter, respectively, soon followed. The energy we felt on stage was transported to the audience and their energy back to us. The performance became a happening. Such happenings are seldom shared between students and administrators and that is a shame. These students gave me the experience I was searching for decades earlier at the Brill Building.

Father Bagley became a Monsignor, but he never forgot to visit his boys on the West Side. We finally became of age and could now visit these landmark clubs by simply paying the cover at the door. I've got to confess, nothing beat the thrill of sneaking in. Years later we found out that Tom was actually the great recording engineer Tom Dowd. He lived on Riverside Drive just steps away from the park where we would often practice our crooning. While at Atlantic Records, Tom Dowd worked with the likes of Ray Charles, Aretha Franklin, Eric Clapton and countless others. Ian graduated that June and went on to one of the prestigious music schools in the northeast.

Chapter III

Mrs. Gianna Torentino was a young reading specialist I had taken under my wing when she joined our staff three years earlier. Gianna was a natural. She understood that the most fundamental of questions had to be asked and asked first when attempting to teach. How does this child learn? She understood that differentiating instruction was not enough. Differentiated instruction is a hit or miss proposition. Mrs. Torentino knew that in order for one to tap into a student's learning capacity, one has to understand how the student perceives and processes information. She opened her mind and heart to her students and her results were remarkable. Whether it was direct instruction, creativity, discovery or small group, Mrs. Torentino instinctively knew what method to apply and how to apply it. Very often a teacher appears but the student isn't ready. The student isn't ready because he hasn't been awakened. Gianna Torentino knew how to motivate and awaken a student; that was the key to her success.

This enthusiastic reading specialist scheduled an after-school conference the same day as the Villanueva conference, which was weighing heavily on my mind. The woman that walked in my office was not the smiling, bubbling master teacher I was accustomed to speaking with, but a depressed individual whose spirit had been broken. I knew something was painfully wrong. It's not often that a teacher or anyone confides their inner most feelings and personal life with an immediate supervisor. Unaware, I had developed a sense of trust. My favorite teacher needed advice and with tears in her eyes proceeded to share her hurt. Gambling is a habit that could drain an individual to the point of desperation. Homes have been lost, savings squandered and lives totally destroyed by gambling. Infidelity kills trust, the foundation for all relationships, partnerships and marriages, Gianna's husband had pierced her heart with both these swords. Somehow this situation was all too familiar but back then I was on the other side of the desk.

Saint Bernard Annex to Cardinal Hayes High School was where I found myself in the fall of 1963, and let me tell you, right from the start; Christian Brothers slapped the shit out of people. They must have taken a special course or some type of in-service training because these guys mastered the art of slapping you silly. There was no detention, suspension or intervention. If you stepped out of line, you would get your bell rung and problem solved. If you or your parents didn't like it, you could leave and go to public school. My mother loved that philosophy. All the parents loved that philosophy. In fact, as long as you were not the one getting smacked, it was rather entertaining. Watching a grown man in a robe, chasing a teenager, around the classroom as the teenager yelled, "No! Brother, please! Brother" was a sight to behold. Claudio Rappaport got his ass kicked every day. If it wasn't for not having homework, it was for arriving late to school. If it wasn't for arriving late to school, it was for cutting class. Finally, the Brothers figured it out. Rappaport was not allowed to play football. Overnight Claudio Rappaport became a changed young man. Football was his passion, so Claudio vowed to conform, and he did.

"Mr. Gigante, would you like to help with this experiment?"

"Sure Brother!"

Bam!!! He never saw it coming. He was too busy bullshitting and not paying attention to the experiment. Brother Vincent knocked him into the following week. Gigante got an "A" on every other experiment the rest of freshman year.

Brother Patrick had a Barber's Strap. He never used the strap, Brother didn't have to. He simply walked into class, dropped the strap on his desk and all eyes were front. Brother Patrick never had a problem with students being engaged in the lesson or being focused on the assignment. In fact, if you weren't paying attention—you made believe you were. The Christian Brothers education was probably the single most positive influence I have had in my life other than my mother. Being a single parent raising three boys on the West Side was no easy task. My mother knew that she needed men to make men out of her sons. The Christian Brothers were her answer, and yes they were. The truth is those smacks were few and far between. What we all received was a development of knowledge and more importantly, a thirst for that knowledge. We received a development of character. We were taught to interact with ideas and experiences. It was not merely the acquisition of information and its assessment, which seems to be the only focus today. Although we as students had to conform to the rules and guidelines of the school, the Brothers were humanistic in their approach and tended to the needs of their students and families. The brothers were always there for whatever problem you had, academic or personal.

Hayes was my high school of choice. It was the school I wanted to play baseball for. One of the older guys from the neighborhood played for Hayes. Hayes players wore these satin cardinal red jackets that said class and at the same time intimidated. It's amazing how something as simple as a jacket could leave an impression on a young mind. I didn't want to go to the high school on the West Side, Commerce High School. Commerce was the home of Lou Gehrig, Louie Lefkowitz, Abraham Beam, Cal Ramsey and many more prominent New Yorkers. Yet, my heart said, "leave the West Side and go down to the Hayes Annex in Chelsea". Hayes had its share of prominent grads Regis Philbin, Martin Scorsese, Kevin Loughery. George Carlin attended Hayes for a while before he got booted out. Word was he drove the Priests and Brothers crazy. His skit, "Religion Is Bullshit", demonstrates what he must have put them through.

1963 marked the beginning of the end for my friends and me, as far as hanging out in the neighborhood. We all chose different high schools to attend and through sports, music or clubs we became involved in school life. The weekends gave us the only opportunity to get together and raise a little hell. Hell is what we caught when we got busted one morning in late November, hosting a crap game. The managers of the Riviera Theater on 96st and Broadway decided that they would run "Guys and Dolls", the 1955 hit starring Marlon Brando, Frank Sinatra and Jean Simmons. It was right after sitting through "Guys and Dolls" for the third time one Sunday afternoon that we decided to make some big money. "We can do this" Tommy said. "Do what?" "Run our own crap games in the neighborhood".

Plans were made and we started hosting our own roving crap games. Whether it was up on a roof, down a basement or the back of the Chinese laundry, we always had a packed house. We never had to gamble, the cover charge and 10% of each pot was enough for all of us. The rules were simple: no one over 18 was allowed; no women were allowed; "Cee-Lo" (three dice) was the game with a pot limit of $100; winner takes the pot. We ran our games weekend after weekend with no one knowing where until that night. The cops knew what we were doing, they just didn't know where or when. We thought we were the Nathan Detroits of the West Side, and for a while we were. It was just like the musical but little did we know that we were about to jump from an exciting overture to a punishing finale. We knew the "heat" was on, so we decided to hold a Friday morning crap game which meant everyone had to cut school, bad decision. Truant officers were now out in full force as the twenty-five or so regulars at our games had not reported to school. Little Willie got picked up and he spilled his guts. "Come here you little fuck, where is everybody?" "They are in the 92st subway station". The subway station was closed years earlier and pretty much abandoned, abandoned by everyone except us. The 92st station was one of our favorite spots, easy to get to and easy to leave. Suddenly, cops were everywhere and as the song goes we had "nowhere to run, nowhere to hide". At first we thought it was the typical, "alright get the hell out of here and don't come back", but not this time. This time we had gone too far. We heard the sergeant radio for the paddy wagons and our hearts dropped. This time it was a real bust. Finger prints, mug shots and the one phone call were staring us right in the face. The phone call home was the call I couldn't make. I was ready to deal with whatever punishment, I deserved it, but, I knew the call would break my mother's heart. I called Brother Patrick from Cardinal Hayes High School instead. Brother Patrick knew me from Holy Name Grammar School and like Officer John Doherty and Father Bagley, Brother Pat had my ultimate trust and respect. I needed him to call my mom. It was now early afternoon and we found ourselves in a holding cell when suddenly one of the officers we had nicknamed Batman opened the cell and said; "Go home". The look on his face told us something was terribly wrong but were afraid to ask. We got to the front desk to retrieve our belongings and we saw all these tough cops from the 24th precinct crying. These big predominantly Irish cops were staring at the television and crying like babies. It was then that we learned Kennedy was killed. Upon hearing the news, the captain ordered our release. We were stunned. We couldn't move, we just stood there with these cops, most of whom we knew, listening to the report of the president's assassination. November 22, 1963 was in many ways the day the cloak of innocence was removed from our lives and things were never the same again. We had dodged a situation that would have cost us heavily. Some mistakes you continue to pay for the rest of your life and a police record would have been one of those mistakes. We were given a pass. The Kennedy Assassination was the introduction to a series of events that made even a group of street kids question; who or what was really controlling the country?

I arrived home that afternoon to find Brother Patrick consoling my mom. I remember him holding her hand and looking at me as he quietly said, "good boys are not immune to mistakes". Mom had been served a double dagger that day; her son was picked up by the police and the death of her beloved President, John Fitzgerald Kennedy. I never felt so ashamed. I was ashamed because I knew the sacrifices the woman had made for her three boys. Though not formally educated, she was a woman blessed with many attributes, talents and gifts; however, she was not blessed in marriage. Twice abandoned and alone, she took on the monumental task of raising a son who had a baseball craze, another son who was a stellar student and a third son who was attracted to all the vices the streets had to offer. Ashamed because the three jobs she held in order to afford her boys a parochial school education deserved a better payoff.

Gianna, in her veil of tears, kept repeating, "I don't know what to do". Part of me wanted to say leave the son of a bitch, as I came around from behind my desk. But, her love for this man was obvious and a comment like that and several others I had on my mind would not have solved the problem. Oddly enough, I found myself holding her hand and saying; "Good husbands are not immune to mistakes, let's get the two of you some counseling". I knew the trust issue would be the ultimate hurdle and the one she couldn't overcome. Two years later the Torentinos went their separate ways.

Brother Patrick eventually left the order and went to work for the NYC Board of Education. Forty years later we ran into each other at a Hayes reunion. Seeing him brought tears of joy.

Chapter IV

In all my years I have seen my share of mistakes and God knows I have made some. It's just when these mistakes were made by adults and done because they claimed their actions were in the best interest of kids, was when I lost faith in parenting. Yet, very often a special providence seemed to make things right. Veronica Collazo was the toughest and most volatile fourteen year-old girl I had ever met, she had to be. It was her way of keeping predators at bay. Veronica was pretty and flirtatious. Veronica was an early bloomer. Veronica was a victim of parental child abuse. Her step-father believed the only path to curfew observance was beating her mercilessly. "Mr. Francisco, would you like to read my essay? The title is, "Goldie Locks and the Three Bears Revisited". This was Veronica's way of saying, look at me, look what my step-father did to me. Through the emotional and physical pain, she immediately jumped to the end and moral of the story which had an inner-city twist, "just like in the ghetto, bears need to keep their damn doors locked". She laughed through her tears and that gave me the opportunity to casually ask about the welts on her arms and swollen cheek. Veronica put her head down and said, "do what you have to do, I can't take it any more". A social worker from the Department of Youth and Family Services was in my office within the hour. Veronica Collazo was removed from her step-father's home and placed in foster care. The impact this family had on Veronica was miraculous, a type of "Divine Intervention". Unlike many abused teenagers who experience delinquency, drug addiction, alcoholism, teen pregnancy and low academic achievement, Veronica immersed herself in school life. Veronica became an excellent soccer player and captain of the team her senior year. She tapped into that inner toughness and tenacity and became a constant on the principal's honor roll. Her college essay praised and thanked her new family for saving her life. Veronica now speaks three languages and is pursuing a law degree at the University of Buffalo.

Eli Barrett's uncle decided he was going to act in Eli's best interest the day he convinced the impressionable youth he could make good money selling weed in school. My heart broke the moment I watched this good student-athlete escorted out of the building in hand cuffs. The charge was possession with intent to sell. Eli looked at me and asked if I could get him off the hook but at that point there was nothing I could do. We had set up a stake out near the library which was just opposite the boy's bathroom. We were acting on an anonymous tip. The last student we suspected of such activity was Eli Barrett. A plain clothed officer who was twenty-four and didn't look a day over sixteen made the bust. I followed the squad car down to the station and met the parents there. The Eli incident was particularly disturbing because The Barretts had all the pieces to the drug prevention puzzle in place; strong parental support, involvement and guidance. Eli was a D.A.R.E. graduate, honor student and varsity athlete. If such temptation could attract an Eli Barrett, it could attract anyone if the price is right; your son, my son, the preachers daughter. Unfortunately for the Barrett Family the fox was in the hen house. Eli never "ratted" on the uncle who never stepped up. Years later, the uncle was arrested for soliciting a sixteen year-old prostitute. Somehow sins always revisit in one form or another.

Today, Eli teaches English and is one of the top basketball coaches in the state.

I was sixteen when the craziest of all my uncles but the one I loved most, decided he was going to act in my best interest. It was time for me to become a man. It was wonderful how my five uncles looked after different aspects of our lives, not having a Dad and all. My brothers and I always had someone to take us for haircuts, take us to ball games, take us to the Apollo Theater or even give us a kick in the ass whenever we needed it. We were on our way back from Yankee Stadium when my uncle Freddy, whose real name was Pablo Antonio Garcia y Valdez, asked me if I had ever been with a girl. How a name like that wound up being Freddy I don't know. God knows what made him pop that question. I said, "Yes! Are you kidding me?" He laughed and said, "I don't mean making out with some of those little hussies on the block; oh yea, I see you sneaking down the basement. I mean, have you ever been in bed with a woman?" I really didn't want to talk about it and didn't want to tell him the truth. I proudly replied, "Yes". He knew I was lying. "That's it we're going to Maxine's". By now, Maxine was the prettiest, hottest woman on the West Side. Maxine was not just turning tricks. She was a shrewd business woman and her profession was "The Oldest Profession". The Four Seasons Barber Shop on Manhattan Avenue was just a front. Now don't get me wrong, you got a great hair cut at the Four Seasons; Angelo, Pat and Vito were great barbers. But, if you were part of the right clientele, a haircut is not all you got. Men would come from all over town for a haircut, a shave and whatever else was on the menu. My brothers and I were not allowed to get haircuts at The Four Seasons. We had to go to Armando's on 96st. We never questioned why, because we knew what was going on and felt out of our league anyway. Well, Freddy decided that it was time for me to move up to the "Majors". It was late in the afternoon as we walked down the avenue. I felt like I was on my way to the dentist, not on my way to having a woman for the first time. Whenever I was able to convince Pookie or one of the other girls to meet me up on the roof, down the basement or at the movies, there was a sense of excitement. This walk felt as though I was going to have a tooth pulled, but, I couldn't let my uncle know how nervous I was. All he kept talking about was how he had his first woman in Cuba when he was fifteen. I really didn't give a shit who he banged in Cuba. Since I was twelve all I heard from the women in the neighborhood was stay away from the Four Seasons and Maxine. I couldn't wait to go to the Four Seasons, the women were wrong about everything else. Now with the moment at hand, all I felt was fear. My fear was two-fold, performance or the lack there of and getting caught. On occasion some had been caught by their wives or girlfriends. "Fat Joe Moe" got caught. To see a pot bellied old man in his underwear running down the avenue with his wife chasing him with a barber's razor was simply choice. Uncle Freddy and I walked into The Four Seasons Barbershop and my uncle told Angelo the barber that I was there for my first shave. Now at sixteen, I was already shaving. Angelo knew what Freddy meant and went in the back to talk to Maxine. Meanwhile, I took a seat as though I was waiting for a haircut. All these men, some who I knew and some who I didn't care to know, kept smiling at me and nodding their heads with approval. I was embarrassed. No, I was too nervous to be embarrassed. I didn't know what I was. Suddenly, the curtain that led to the back softly slid open and there stood Maxine. Maxine had this Look. Maxine's Look was different. It was this Liz Taylor Look. She glanced at me and said, "Come on back". Time was suspended. I don't recall whether it took me fifteen seconds or fifteen minutes to walk fifteen feet. I stepped into what was and still remains, the most beautiful parlor I have ever seen. One couldn't believe that crystals, paintings and plush rugs could be found on Manhattan Avenue. Maxine gently grabbed my hand and led me to her bedroom which was also a sight to behold, mirrors, pillows and a king sized bed. Maxine was as patient and gentle as any woman in this situation could possibly be. She said, "The pants have to come off". So I did, take the pants off. Now I was not only nervous but cold. I was shaking like a leaf. Maxine reclined on the bed, grabbed my hand and said; "Now, you just climb on". So I "climbed on". I wasn't supposed to literally "climb on" but for some reason, I did. My knee hit her in the eye and knocked her eyelash off. For the life of me, I can't begin to explain what my knee was doing up by her eye but there it was and Maxine was pissed. I had exhausted her patience and the "real" Maxine, the tom-boy Maxine came out. "Mother Fucker, you gotta go and take your dopey uncle with you". I rushed my pants on, stepped into the barbershop and said, "Freddy, we've gotta go". I never told my friends but somehow they found out I was at the Four Seasons. The truth was never told. My simple reply was, "it's private" and with a smile. In a way I did take a step towards becoming a man that day. I realized what was missing, the "prelude", that Astaire-Rogers moment when you fall for a girl, girl resists, girl finally says yes to the "dance", girl lets you lead her through the "dance", girl falls for you, while you're dancing. Whether it's an innocent glance, a first date or weeks of courtship, nothing beats the prelude to a conquest, except the conquest.

Despite being misguided by what we will call overambitious adults, things turned out well for Veronica, Eli and me, thanks to that special providence that sometimes appears in The School of Hard Knocks.

Chapter V

My one-hundred and eighty days as principal were coming to an end as were my thirty-seven years as a teacher, coach and administrator. My prelude to what could have been a renaissance for our high school was ending in the manner it had ended for my predecessor and exactly as I had predicted, an "early autumn". The "power elite's" ambition was to have an administrator who would front their goal, the calculated takeover of the school district. Contrary to promoting success for all students, collaborating with community leaders and responding to the needs of the diverse district population, the focus was directing all efforts and resources to the "power elite's" own self-serving, political agenda. Although the climate at the school had changed and the morale among students and faculty was high, my requests for changing the structure of the school and establishing career academies had fallen on deaf ears. The strategies I had suggested for improving student engagement and truly addressing learning styles and instruction were thought to be unpractical. Providing student incentives for participation in after-school tutoring programs ruffled feathers in the board of education and in the community. "Students should not be given incentives to prepare for the state exam". That statement I didn't understand. Were not those scores our most pressing need? Districts are measured by how students score on these high powered tests. What is a scholarship, if not an incentive? In a sense, a scholarship is a reverse mortgage, money awarded for years of academic investment. What I was proposing was an investment in our kids. Mortgage students as well as the teachers incentives up front and demand effort and productivity. Similar strategies have proven successful in urban communities around the country. The truth of the matter was that the district refused to put its money in its mission statement.

June was upon us and I found myself presiding over graduation at Abraham Lincoln High School. My farewell address was based on the values I had learned at home, in academia and in life "The School of Hard Knocks".

"Shortly I will discharge my last duties as Principal of Abraham Lincoln High School. My one-hundred and eighty days of service to the students and faculty have been an honor and privilege".

You now have the challenge of entering the world at a time many feel is the most difficult since the Great Depression, a harsh time in our history. Not so, "this time, like all times is a very good one" as Emerson said, "if we know what to do with it". It is a time for high ideals, strong ambition in the service of your fellow-man. Remember that nature has formed you and Wisdom will preserve you.

Go slow but sure, it breeds conviction.

Learn well. Education is a lifelong experience.

Beware of those who expel and reject whom they please. Their house is self-serving.

Dare to be great. Strength, confidence and valor are born from it.

Trust that Wisdom preserves those who seek happiness from within, not in how they have satisfied themselves but how they have served others. Love humanity, for you were put on this earth to make it a better place.

As I watched my last class of graduates celebrate among themselves, parents, younger brothers and sisters, I asked myself as Mr. Chips did, "where did my childhood go"?

Epilogue

In August, the chief administrator for the school district was not issued a contract and the fourth superintendent of schools in six years was sworn in.

Edwards Brothers,Inc!
Thorofare, NJ 08086
08 November, 2010
BA2010313